FRIENDS
OF ACPL

Candle in the Sky

By the same Author

SUNFLIGHT

THE CRUSADE AND THE CUP

EST·1852

Candle in the Sky

Elizabeth Bleecker Meigs

ILLUSTRATED BY DOROTHY BAYLEY MORSE

NEW YORK · E. P. DUTTON & CO., INC. · 1953

FOR BILL

CONTENTS

Author's Note

This is the story of a girl. Many of the things that I have written about her are true things. I am a story-teller. This is how I imagined it would have been if Jean de Metz was the sort of person I have written about, and if Joan, the Maid of Orleans, was like the girl in this story.

Candle in the Sky

Chapter I — The Pledge

JEAN DE NOVELOMPONT REINED UP SHARPLY. THE GRAY
stallion reared under him as the barbed French bits
caught in the sensitive hinge of his jaw. His hind legs
skidded on the wet cobbles. Jean laid a hand on the
corded muscles of his neck.

"Gently now. Gently. We are nearly come to the level." At the sound of his voice, husky and persuasive, the stallion quieted.

"Bertrand?" The young man turned in his saddle. One hand rested lightly on the gray's rump.

"I am with you, Jean. Wait, I beg of you, until we are indeed come to the level. Inasmuch as that beast you ride is possessed of the temper of Satan, it will be safer for my lady here."

Jean laughed. "Your lady is old and her bones are brittle with many seasons of war."

His companion shrugged. As they clattered down the narrow causeway that led from the governor's castle of Vaucouleurs into the market place, Bertrand de Poulengy brushed the flanks of his chestnut mare with gilded spurs. Obediently she surged abreast of the stallion.

"She has done me good and knightly service. Without her I would not have come alive from the field of Rouvray in the month that is gone."

Jean turned to him. His face was spare and serious in the failing twilight. The laughter quenched in his dark eyes.

"Rouvray was disaster. Unless the siege of Orleans is soon lifted, one more such victory for the English will ensnare our people of France, and drive our King from his kingdom."

Bertrand gazed at him strangely. "It is true then?

You believe in this thing that we have seen this afternoon. I felt that you believed in the girl when she stood in front of de Baudricourt."

"I believed."

"Is it when there is nothing left to believe in, that you believe in this? The fair land of France is black with the ashes of burnt villages and ruined manors. The soldiers of our King go unpaid. The people are hungry. Small wonder that the English and their allies of Burgundy turn them from their allegiance to the crown of France."

Jean reined the prancing stallion down to a walk. He breathed deeply. The familiar stench of refuse thrown into the gutterless streets mingled with the clear scent of new-fallen snow borne on the north wind. He looked back over his shoulder at the castle, its towers hunched black against the blue onslaught of evening. He wondered if there were words to tell how it was with him. He thought that Bertrand was his brother in arms. They had sworn brotherhood on the field of battle when the English invaded Lorraine. Both young knights were in the service of René the Duke of Bar, and Jean had saved the life of his friend, parrying the blow of an English mace with his own ax, when Bertrand's horse stumbled beneath him. He thought of that day, and the smell of blood, raw disconsolate smell, was in his nostrils again, as he thought. He searched for the words.

"It is not that there is nothing left to believe in. It is not that. It is something else. Something has been given to us today. I think it is hope."

"Hope?"

"Yes. When the girl Joan stood in front of the governor, as she spoke, Bertrand, I felt hope for our land, for our people, for our King, even as she pledged."

"What gave you this hope, my friend?"

"I do not know. She stood straight as a lance in her red woolen dress. Perhaps that was it. . . . Perhaps it was her hands when she told de Baudricourt to send her to the King because her Lord commanded it. She turned her hands down. Something eloquent and final in that gesture. . . ." He broke off.

Suddenly the gray stallion reared as the knees of his master tightened against his foreflanks.

"Bertrand, I am going to help Joan. I am going now to find her. I will bring her to the place where the King is."

"To Chinon? It is a distance of three hundred and fifty miles, my friend. The territory between Vaucouleurs and Chinon is infested with English and Burgundians. There are three rivers to cross and it is mid-winter." Bertrand de Poulengy smiled as he spoke.

"You will ride with me?"

"Of course, Jean."

"Then let us find her now. Do you know where in the town she is lodged?"

"She is lodged in the house of Henri le Royer the wheelwright. I will show you the way."

Bertrand wheeled his mare and cantered down one of the narrow alleys that led from the market place. There were few people abroad at this hour, for with the going down of the sun, the townspeople were accustomed to barring their doors for the night. The horses' iron-shod hoofs rang lonely on the slush-mired cobblestones.

Half a mile from the square, Bertrand reined up before a small house that was wedged tightly between two others. The door was barred. A faint gleam of light from the uneven joining of the threshold and the oaken door indicated the presence of the family within.

The two young men dismounted in silence. In silence they looked at one another. Abruptly Jean rapped on the solid oak. Bertrand took the bridles of their horses and tethered them to an iron ring set in the wall of the house.

"Who knocks at this unseemly hour?"

"Jean de Novelompont, a knight in the service of the King."

The bolts slid back. Creaking on its hinges, the narrow door opened. Jean bent his head and stepped down into the room. The ceiling was low. The soot-blackened beams forced him to keep his head bent. Bertrand stepped in behind him.

Henri le Royer bolted the door. His wrinkled face was quizzical with unexpressed wonder as he pulled his gray forelock with the immemorial gesture of the peasant in homage to those of gentle blood. The young men were clad in straight woolen garments, Jean's a vivid blue and Bertrand's a dark green. Their padded surcoats were of black velvet bordered with miniver and secured at their waists with belts of heavy leather. They wore no armor save the traditional sword, which together with the gilded spurs was the badge of their knighthood.

Smoky golden shadows danced on the walls cast by the firelight. On a table stood a jug of soured wine. In the denser shadow by the hearth, two women sat spinning. The elder wore a brown woolen dress with the heavy overskirt that the bitter cold made necessary. Her face like her husband's was wrinkled, but her hair was completely hidden beneath the folds of her white linen coif.

The firelight touched the red skirt of her companion, and caught the shining length of her black hair, braided into a thick single plait. It swung over her shoulder as she lifted her face to the visitors. Impatiently she shook it back. She glanced quickly at Madame le Royer.

Then she rose and crossed the room to where Jean and Bertrand stood. She held out a hand to each of them. Her hands like her face were brown from exposure to wind and sun. Her eyes beneath thick black brows were the color of sea water, and when she smiled suddenly, it was like the touch of sunlight on the gray sea.

"You were in the castle hall this afternoon when the governor refused to send me to the King."

"Yes," Bertrand said.

"I am Jean de Novelompont. Men call me Jean de Metz." He held fast to the hand she had given him. He gazed down at her, a fathomless pity in his dark eyes.

"Joan," he said, "Joan, what do you do here? Shall the King be driven from the kingdom? Shall we indeed become English?"

The girl looked at him. She shook her head violently. "Sir Knight, I came to this town of Vaucouleurs to tell Robert de Baudricourt to send me to the King. But he heeds neither me or my words. Today he laughed at me again. You heard him. Nonetheless, before mid-Lent is come, I must be on my way to the King, if I must walk to Chinon. For nobody"—again she shook her black head—"nobody can succor the kingdom. Only I can. It would be better to spend the winter days spinning by the side of my mother in our village of Domremy, as I do here"—she nodded in the direction of Catherine le Royer who sat quietly by the spinning wheel—"seeing that these things do not belong in my station. I am a peasant maid, not the daughter of a King. Yet I must go, for my Lord has willed it."

Jean's grasp on her hand tightened. "Who is your Lord?"

"The King of Heaven is my Lord." Her clear, deep voice rang with conviction.

"Joan, I will take you to the King. With the help of God, I will take you. To this I pledge my knightly word."

Joan turned white. Then the color surged into her cheeks lending her a strange beauty. Her eyes were wet. It was too much, and it happened so suddenly after the months of delay and ridicule. She looked up into Jean's dark eyes, and smiled.

"When do you wish to set out, Joan?" Bertrand asked gently.

She turned to him laughing. "Now."

"But surely—"

"No," she interrupted him, "now rather than tomorrow, but tomorrow rather than the day following."

"Joan, it will be a difficult journey, and we must prepare for it well." Jean released her hand and stared critically at her lithe figure in the red woolen dress. "You cannot go like that. . . ."

She flushed.

"Would you consent to dress as a man?"

"Willingly."

"Your hair too. That must be shorn."

She nodded. From her corner by the hearth, Catherine le Royer stifled an exclamation of horror.

"Tomorrow, Joan, we will bring you such clothing as you shall require. We will bring you boots. Can you ride?"

Joan smiled. "I have ridden the horses in our village. Such beasts are used in the heavy labor of plowing. I have ridden them to pasture. But I have never ridden with a saddle. . . ."

The young men exchanged an amused glance.

"We will try to find you a good and gentle mount," Bertrand said.

"When shall we leave?" Joan looked urgently from one to the other.

"As soon as these things are accomplished. Joan, you have been patient until now. You told the governor that you had waited for seven years obeying the commands of Saint Michael and Saint Margaret and Saint Catherine in all things until the time was ripe, and they bade you set forth. Now the time is indeed come. But you must be patient a little longer," Jean finished gravely. "Until we have collected the gear for your journey. Two of our friends, Richard the Archer and Colet de Vienne who is a messenger of the King, are in Vaucouleurs at this time. They will be returning to Chinon on the twenty-third of February. We will ride with them, Joan, for your greater protection."

"That is ten days hence!" she exclaimed.

"Truly." Jean smiled. "And I pledge you, Joan, that on the evening of that day we will set forth. God helping me, I will bring you even as I have said to Chinon where the King abides."

She looked at him steadily for a moment. Then her dark young face lighted with a smile of such compelling tenderness that Jean turned aside.

"God helping you," Joan said, "you can do no other."

Chapter II—The Journey

AN EARLY WINTER SUNSET CRIMSONED THE TOWERS OF
Vaucouleurs and streaked the snow clouds banked on
the western horizon.

In the courtyard of the governor's castle, seven
horses were being readied for a journey.

Robert de Baudricourt stood by the head of a stocky Flemish gelding. One hand toyed nervously with the hilt of his sword. With the other, he was holding the bridle rein. His lifted face entreated the girl who sat astride the horse.

"Perhaps you are mad. Or perhaps I am mad to let you ride out of this gate. But if you are indeed sent by God to succor the Kingdom of France, then God watch over you on your journey. For it is like to be a perilous one. I have brought you a sword," he concluded roughly. He jerked his head in the direction of a page who stood behind him. The boy came up. He bowed to the governor and extended a sword sheathed in a plain leather scabbard, its hilt embossed with silver fleurs-de-lis. It was attached to a heavy leather belt with a silver buckle. De Baudricourt reached up and buckled it around her slim waist. Joan touched the hilt. Then she reached her lean brown hand to the governor. She did not thank him. She smiled. There was something in that smile of the strange, almost radiant tenderness that had caused Jean de Metz to turn his head.

"You are not mad, Sire Robert. And I do not fear this journey. The way is made open to me. My Lord will know. He will make straight the path that leads to the King. It is for this I was born." De Baudricourt stepped back. Jean de Metz trotted up on his gray stallion. He leaned over and snapped a lead on the gelding's bridle. He saluted the governor.

"We are ready, Sire Robert."

De Baudricourt was still looking at Joan. It was as if he had not heard the young knight. He said to her,

"Go. Go then. Let it be as God wills." With a fatalistic shrug, he turned on his heel and strode from the courtyard.

The portcullis had been raised. The King's messenger and his friend, Richard the Archer, rode out. Bertrand de Poulengy closed in on Joan's left. Behind them, their two squires rode, the extra cloaks and the food lashed in leather sacks to the high cantles of their saddles.

Away westward the sunset which had touched the clouds with its fiery, transient beauty faded. The landscape darkened. Forest and snow-crowned hills blended in that darkness. The steep road that led from the castle gate was little better than a cart track filled with water holes left by the recent snowfall.

Cautiously, the little band descended.

Joan straightened in her saddle. She looked over her shoulder just once, at the black towers of Vaucouleurs. Bertrand saw her lips move.

"What were you thinking, Joan?"

"I was thinking of my mother. In Domremy, this is the hour of the evening bread. I prayed for her. . . ."

Bertrand stretched out a hand. At that consoling touch, she looked at him in astonishment.

"Joan, are you sure? Even now, it is not too late. We could take you home to your mother."

Joan shook her black head as she had shaken it on the night they had first spoken to her.

"It would be better to spend the days spinning by her side; even I have told you. But for this I was born and I must go because my Lord has willed it." She hesitated, smiling a little. "Even this I was commanded to do." She touched her bare head and glanced down at the sword that hung by her side.

"You are a fine boy, surely," Jean teased. He smiled at Bertrand. "Only one thing we have forgotten, my friend. We have forgotten to give her a cap."

"I shall not need one. I am not cold."

Both knights laughed.

"Joan, Joan, the night air will harm you. No man rides abroad without a head covering of some kind. And you who only yesterday had hair of a full yard's length..."

"I am not cold," she repeated, "but if no man rides abroad without a head covering, and I am to act the part of a man, then I will wear a cap."

Jean reached into the leather bag that depended from the cantle of his saddle. He pulled out a black woolen page's cap and handed it to her.

Joan set it squarely on her head and then glanced

inquiringly from one to the other of her cavaliers. They nodded in unison. For a time they rode in silence, each of them enmeshed in secret thought.

Joan loosened her knees and arched her back to ease it from the unaccustomed strain of her position. The black hose and gray tunic felt as alien to her body as the heavy riding boots and the chafing weight of the sword at her waist. Unconsciously she tossed her head, but the weight of her thick black braid was gone. The hair was cut in an uneven fringe across her brow and cropped like a boy's just below her ears.

Darkness mantled the earth. The north wind quickened. Snow fell. Wet, stinging snow that got in the eyes and packed the hoofs of the horses.

Jean pulled his fur-lined cloak from his shoulders and wrapped it about the girl. She looked at him with her radiant smile.

"Joan, have you ever swum a horse through a stream? Do you know what it is like?"

"No, I have never done that."

"There are four rivers between Vaucouleurs and Saint Urbain's Monastery which is the first place we will halt. We should reach it with the daybreak."

"When do we come to the first river?"

"Now. A mile beyond Saulx Village runs the river of the same name. Are you afraid?"

"Will I be very wet when we are done with the crossing of these rivers?"

"Very wet and very cold."

"Then it is very well," Joan said contentedly. "For these are the things a man must do. And if I am to learn the ways of a man, it would be better to learn quickly, would it not?" She smiled at both of them.

Jean made no answer; he merely tightened his hold on the lead attached to her bridle.

The sound of water rushing over rocks echoed disconsolate on the north wind. They rode down a steep embankment, the skittish stallion half reared as the icy current swirled about his fetlocks. His master raked him with his spurs, forcing him into the dark water. Bertrand eased his mare into the river and kept her close to Joan as the three horses began to swim, heads thrust out, the water closing over their backs. Drenched to the skin and shivering with cold, the three surged up the opposite bank.

Joan smiled from one young man to the other.

"It is indeed cold, but it is not so difficult as I thought, to swim a horse." Her teeth were chattering.

Colet de Vienne, the King's messenger, brought a wine flask from his saddle bag. He took a hasty gulp and offered it to Bertrand. Bertrand held it out to Joan.

"I do not wish to drink strong wine."

"Drink, Joan. You will have need of all your strength, and if you would truly learn the ways of a man . . ." he let the suggestion trail off.

Obediently, Joan lifted the flask in both hands. She

gulped. The wine was not sour like the thin red vintage she had been accustomed to since childhood. It was dark and rich and sweet and she felt it run like fire through her inward parts, warming her chilled body even as she drank.

She returned the flask to Colet. For a moment they clustered around her, while the flask was handed to the others. Then they wheeled their horses and resumed the original order of march, Jean keeping a firm hand on the leading rein of the girl's horse.

Morning penetrated the forest. It silvered the wet black branches of the trees and touched with an iridescent sheen the new fallen snow. A bell tolled and its silvery voice echoed through the silence.

Joan drew rein. She crossed herself.

"What bell is that?"

"That is the monastery bell of Saint Urbain's."

"We will be there in time for the first mass?"

"Yes."

"That is very well then. I am glad. . . ."

"You should be glad to have some food in your belly, and some dry clothing for your back, too." Colet de Vienne, riding ahead, turned in his saddle and stared with grudging admiration at her.

"You have indeed borne yourself as a man this night."

Bertrand and Jean nodded in agreement. Their admiration made Joan flush with embarrassment.

"Surely I was well instructed," she said, and kicked her horse into a trot.

They clattered into the monastery courtyard as the last silvery notes tolled into silence. The abbot himself came to greet them. He was a tall spare old man. His chill blue eyes softened as he looked at Joan.

"So you are the maid of whom we have heard such rumors in the month that is gone. Come, my child. Come in. When you have heard Mass and broken your fast, we will find for you a place to lie. For you must be very weary."

Joan slid from the saddle and knelt awkwardly to kiss his ring. The sword would have tripped her but for Jean's steadying hand. The muscles of her thighs and her back were numbed with cold and the long hours of riding.

The abbot lifted her up. His hand rested for a moment on her black head, while he searched her face intently.

"Will you surely do what you have said?"

Joan straightened under his hand proudly.

"Lord Abbot, have no fear. What I do, I do by commandment."

"I have no fear, my child," the old man answered gently. "For if you do these things by commandment, there is indeed nothing to fear. Now come in and break

bread with our Lord, whose commandment this is."
Taking her by the hand, he led her into the cloister,
the two knights following at their heels.

Three hundred and thirty miles of the journey lay
behind Joan and her companions. They were traveling
in a country whose sympathies lay with the French
cause. They traveled by day, and avoiding the towns,
they made camp wherever night overtook them.

The earth quickened with the green promise of
spring. The wind blew from the south raw and sweet
with the scents of that quickening.

Joan dismounted wearily. The brief blue twilight
deepened into evening, and the rustling sounds of the
forest were hushed. They had traveled far in the ten
days they had been on the road. Wearily the men examined the hoofs of their horses and unsaddled them,
checking automatically for any signs of girth gall and
sore withers. The spirited gray stallion of Jean de Metz
stood as quietly as Bertrand's old mare under his master's hands. The lean arc of his ribs and the jutting
point of his hip bone were plainly visible in the failing
light. He, as well as the rest of them, was weary.

Jean de Metz spread his military cloak on the
ground.

"Sit, ma mie."

. Gratefully Joan sank to the earth. Bertrand cut with
his dagger a thick wedge of black bread from a loaf

he carried. Colet passed her the wine jug. Joan smiled
at them, too weary for speech. Wrapping her own
mantle close about her she lay flat. Stars began to
silver the night.

Bertrand and Jean threw themselves down on either
side of her. They slept almost immediately. The others
lay in a protecting semicircle around them.

Only Joan did not sleep. Her nerves tensed, she lay
gazing up through the branches of the trees into the
lonely reach of starlit sky.

"Joan."

"Yes? My lady, oh, my lady Margaret, Catherine,
where are you?"

"We are here, Joan." A hot flood of consolation suddenly released the overstrung nerves of the girl. She
twisted on her stomach without disturbing her companions, and got to her knees. In the luminous star-
shine, she saw them standing under the giant oak tree,
close to where she knelt. Her two friends, whose faces
had become more familiar to her over the years than
the faces of her own brothers.

She gazed avidly. Catherine was young. Shining hair
like the hair of a fairy princess fell golden over her
shoulders. When she smiled at Joan, she smiled as a
sister would. Margaret looked from one girl to the
other and her wrinkled countenance became beautiful
with compassion as she looked.

"Joan child. We have come to tell you something.

You must remember it. When the night is dark about you, when there is not one star, then you must remember."

"I will remember it, my lady Margaret." Catherine impulsively reached a hand to her. Joan took the hand and held its living warmth against her brown cheek.

"You will have help, Joan," the girl said. "Believe me, you will have help, but take everything that comes. Do not be afraid. Through a strange victory you will be delivered. And we will bring you into the Kingdom where the King of Heaven is."

As Catherine spoke, a spasm of mortal tenderness crossed the older woman's face. Margaret reached out a hand and pushed the untidy fringe of black hair off Joan's forehead.

"Tomorrow you will be in Chinon, little daughter. They will bring you to the King. Do not be afraid. Only remember what we have said. Now fare you well." Catherine bent and kissed her on the cheek.

Tears gathered in Joan's eyes, blurring the stars over her, the black silence of the forest about her and the figures of her friends as they took their leave.

Spent, she sank back on her heels, touched by the unconditional loneliness of her own heart. They were gone. And the joy that they brought was gone with them. For a moment she remained spent and dejected. Then she looked down at the vulnerable sleeping faces of her two knights. They had lain close against her that their bodies might keep her warm while she slept. Suddenly the consolation that had flooded her being when she heard the voices of her friends call, flooded through her again. The sweat tainted human warmth of Jean and Bertrand comforted her.

Trying not to wake either of them, Joan lay down. She turned on her side, and found herself gazing straight into the dark eyes of Jean de Metz.

"I thought you asleep," she said simply.

"No, Joan." For a moment he lay silent. Feeling obscurely that he had been witness to something that was intensely personal, he apologized. "Joan, I did not mean to watch you while you—prayed. I was awake. And I heard you. It is thus they come to you then? For I saw nothing and I heard nothing. But when you answered, I heard you. Will you indeed do what you have said?" He took both her hands in a grip of such unconscious strength she winced.

"I will, Jean, have no fear." A shadow of the joyous welcome he had seen in her smile when she got to her knees flickered across her face once more. Her use of his Christian name moved him strangely. Suddenly as in a dream he felt a warning touch him.

"Joan," he said urgently. "Joan, listen. This is a great thing you would do. I pledged my knightly word that I would bring you to Chinon. But when the battle is won, when the realm is restored, when our King is crowned, what then?"

"I do not know what then. Only I believe I have not a great deal of time in which to accomplish these things. . . ."

"Joan, if any misfortune should befall, even so, remember that I will be with you. Whatever comes, I will be with you. Remember this."

She gazed at him with a lost smile, the young ardent voice of Catherine echoed strangely through his words.

"I will remember," she promised, as she had promised her friends.

"Tomorrow," he said, "we will be in the City of Chinon and I will bring you into the presence of the King."

Chapter III — The King

IT WAS DARK. THE DARK FLOWING WATERS OF THE RIVER
Vienne reflected back a little of the starry sky. The
castle of Chinon put out the stars, its massive turrets
and battlements rising in black majesty from the hill

above the town, as Joan, escorted by Bertrand de
Poulengy and Jean de Metz, rode into its courtyard.
They were admitted by guards wearing the royal livery. A page carrying a silver candelabra guided them
up the great central staircase. At the top before the
double doors of the King's audience chamber, twelve
men-at-arms clad in scarlet and gold stood at attention.

Joan hesitated. In the shadow play of candlelight
and torchlight, Jean saw her face drained of color. She
trembled, hesitating for the space of a heartbeat on
the threshold of her destiny. He put his hand briefly
over her icy fingers which were clenched around the
hilt of her sword. She looked at him in wordless gratitude. Then she squared her shoulders and followed the
page who threw open the great doors.

Joan and the two young men stood at the entrance
of the chamber. Candles burning in silver sconces
filled it with a blaze of light that was reflected back
from the glittering jewels, the cloth of gold, the ermine, the sapphire velvet and vivid crimson of the
courtiers who thronged the room. The air was heavy
with the mingled scents of musk and cosmetics.

Regnault de Chartres, the Archbishop of Reims,
stepped forward. Joan lifted her gray eyes to his face.
She saw his vicious little mouth tighten between the
dewlaps of flesh that a life of dissipation and indolence
had developed. Then she knelt as he extended a pudgy
hand, and kissed the ring that bore the great seal of

his authority. He wore the seamless garment, symbol
of divine pity. It was made of Lyons velvet and bordered with ermine. Joan gazed at him in astonishment.
She had never seen a priest who looked as the Archbishop looked. In that second she made her first mortal
enemy. De Chartres felt her naïve astonishment like
the thrust of a lance. For one second through her eyes
he saw the thing he had become, how far he was from
the vows he had made to the Lord whose garment was
indeed the symbol of pity.

Jean and Bertrand knelt beside her—then at a lan-
guid motion of the Archbishop's hand they rose to
their feet.

Jean looked about eagerly. He had been presented
to the King before, when he had come to Court several
years earlier with his father. Charles was nowhere to
be seen. Behind de Chartres stood Georges de la Tremouille, the King's chief councilor, who more than
any other man in the dying kingdom wished things to
remain as they were. He had no interest in the misery
and hunger of the French people. He was concerned
only that his own plump body should be well covered,
his own treasury well supplied with gold and he himself stuffed with delicacies from the King's table.
Much of his fortune came from the English and the
Burgundians, who paid him a high price to keep
Charles in a state of miserable inactivity. Tremouille
was a past master at this: his chill, sarcastic tongue

frightened the young King more than the thought of capture by the English. For the King's nature was flexible and he was accustomed to his dependence on the chief councilor.

Bertrand knew Tremouille by sight and he bowed to him. Tremouille was dressed as only a king should dress, in the royal purple, a magnificent chain of hammered gold about his thick neck. It was set with pearls and rubies and emeralds.

Joan glanced at him, puzzled. She could not have said how she knew, but she did know that this man was not the King she had been sent to help. She nodded curtly because she had seen Bertrand salute him. Then to the astonishment of the entire Court she said, "By your leave, Sir," and brushed past him. The courtiers divided as she walked boldly across the great room. In the deep embrasure of a window set in the north wall, she found what she was seeking. A young man dressed in somber black velvet leaned in the embrasure, his blue eyes fixed dreamily on the starry sky beyond the casement.

Joan paused in front of him. "My Lord," she said. He turned and stared at her. His thin sensitive face drained of color. They were of an equal height, and for one second, before she fell at his feet, Joan and the King gazed deeply into each other's souls. Charles stooped and lifted the kneeling girl. He took her hands. The murmuring courtiers grew silent. They had seen her rebuff Tremouille. They had seen her stride confidently ahead of her two companions. How had she known the real King?

"My Lord," she said, "I am come to you in the name of the King of Heaven. I am to raise the Siege of Orleans. I am to drive out the English from your kingdom of France. And I am to lead you to Reims where you shall be crowned." Her clear voice rang in the vaulted chamber. Charles gazed at her, his blue eyes lost their dreaminess, while he continued to hold her hands.

"How shall I know that you are indeed sent by God?"

Joan shook her head impatiently. "Because I have told you. My Lord, what has such a one as I am, to do with crowns and kingdoms and fighting? I am but a peasant maid. If the King of Heaven had not sent me how should I have come to you?"

The King shook his fair head and smiled at her suddenly. "How should you have come to me, indeed? It is a good question. Before we part company, Joan, I think you will have gained such knowledge of crowns and kingdoms and fighting as few men possess."

Joan's gray eyes filled with tears. "My Lord," she stammered, "my Lord," and for a moment Jean who stood just behind her, saw her shoulders tremble with the emotion that would not let her speak. He remembered how boldly she had answered him that night in the house of Henri le Royer, the wheelwright, and how the tears had come, when he pledged his knightly word to bring her to Chinon where the King was.

"I shall last a year, perhaps a little longer. I do not know yet," she said, when she could speak, "therefore let us set ourselves to do good work in that year, my Lord."

"What is it you wish to do, Joan?" the King asked gently.

"I wish soldiers and supplies, so that I may go quickly to relieve the people of Orléans. For they are in very sore distress. My—my voices have told me of these things."

"Your voices?"

"The voices of Saint Catherine and Saint Margaret. It is they who bring the command from the King of Heaven which has been laid upon me."

"How do you know that these are truly the voices of Saint Margaret and Saint Catherine and not the messengers of Satan?"

Again she shook her head impatiently. Jean, standing behind her smiled in spite of himself. He had grown used to Joan's direct way of speech; the shattering casual simplicity with which she referred to her Saints no longer left him incredulous.

Joan frowned, her forehead wrinkled earnestly. "How could it be other than I have said?" The King was silent.

Into his silence Tremouille spoke, his voice like acid.

"My Lord, how do we know that this girl is not mad?"

The King flinched as one awakening from a dream. His smile became hesitant. When he looked at Tremouille, it became apologetic.

Joan looked at Tremouille. A long, measuring look it was. She knew her enemy in that moment. The sound instinct within her gauged the depth of his opposition, and the depth of his influence over the hesitant King. Suddenly one oblique message from her friends, Saint Margaret and Saint Catherine became clear. She looked back at the King.

"My Lord," she said carefully, "I am not mad, neither am I sent by the power of evil. My voices have told me that I shall last a year or perhaps a little longer. Surely if I was sent by Satan himself to work evil for you and for the kingdom of France, no limit would have been set on the time in which these things will be accomplished."

The King nodded. Tremouille, for once at a loss, was silent. The King's eyes met Jean's. There was a faint irony in his smile, as he addressed the chief councilor. "Tremouille," he said, "why should we not at least try? We could send Joan with the necessary men and provisions to Orléans. Dunois," he turned courteously to her, "Dunois is my cousin. He is defending the city in the name of my brother, the Duke of Orléans, who is held prisoner by the English." Joan nodded gravely, as if these things were already familiar to her, but she was too polite to interrupt her King. Charles again turned to Tremouille. He spoke decisively.

"We *will* send Joan with an army, and supplies, to relieve my people of Orleans. Dunois has already heard rumors of the Maid from Lorraine, and he will welcome her."

Jean saw a light come into the girl's eyes as if a thousand candles had been lit within her. Impulsively, she pressed his hand. "When may I start?"

"Why, as soon as the preparations are complete," said Charles, and Tremouille went white with the fear that was in him. The English and the Burgundians had just paid him an enormous sum to prevent the King from sending relief to the city of Orleans. He had convinced Charles that the resistance of Dunois was futile. To send more men and supplies to aid him was to shed French blood and waste money and materiel in a hopeless cause. He saw that Joan had in her passionate sincerity undone his evil work. All that remained for her to do was to expose him to the King, and he would, indeed, be ruined. He tried to think of something. A shadow fell between Charles and Joan. The Archbishop laid his pudgy hand familiarly on his royal master's sleeve. The whole group turned to him with the reverence that was instinctive in each of their hearts for the Church his priestly garment represented.

De Chartres rescued Tremouille from his dilemma. He said, "If you were indeed sent to deliver supplies

in Orleans how, even with an army could you hope
to reach the city? The English hold all the great forts
surrounding it, and the number of English troops that
garrison those forts is enormous."

Joan looked at him in surprise. "In God's name, we
shall convey the supplies to Orléans without trouble."
She shook her head with something of the old violence.
"Not one, not one single English soldier will venture
from the forts to detain us. I know."

The Archbishop laughed. "My Lord," he said to the
King. "If this be not midsummer frenzy, then at least
you should wait until Holy Church has examined the
girl thoroughly, lest she has indeed trafficked with the
Evil One."

Joan looked at the King in desperation. But he was
nodding slowly. "It shall be as you have said. Gather
such learned men of the Church as you deem necessary. Examine the girl. But—" he smiled at Joan, and
in his smile, the faith her entreaty had kindled still
lingered.

"But what, my Lord?" Tremouille's voice was indul-
gent, faintly contemptuous even. Charles had again
been prevented from making an immediate decision.
Time had been gained. Time was Tremouille's friend,
his greatest weapon. The King had an almost prehen-
sile sensitivity about other people. He understood both
the indulgence and the contempt. He did not trouble
himself about their origin. Tremouille was always like

that. He hated Tremouille sometimes in his secret heart, but he depended on him to run the kingdom, while he escaped the reality and the responsibility of being King, in his endless daydreams.

"But," he repeated softly, "when the Church has done with its examining, we will gather an army and Joan shall ride with it to Orleans."

Tremouille stared. The Archbishop was plainly startled. He said stupidly to Joan, "What need has God of soldiers?"

Her answer rang through the crowded room. "In God's name, the soldiers will fight and God will give the victory." She looked directly at the King as she spoke, then she looked down, flushing at her own boldness. The King was silent. His face blazed with excitement.

"In God's name then, get on with the examination, your Grace." He turned from the Archbishop to his chief councilor. "And you, Tremouille, collect the necessary supplies, and gather the fighting men, as quickly as possible. I myself will write to Dunois. I will tell him that help is nigh."

Tremouille bowed. There was nothing else to do. Later perhaps, when the King was alone, he could undermine the faith that Joan had kindled . . . but for the present, he could only do as the King commanded. It came to him with an acute sense of shock that he had never heard Charles make a decision, or give a command before. He looked at Joan and her two knights with venom.

Jean de Metz still held the girl's hand. He thought that Joan's coming affected the King in the same way that the stagnant musk and rose-scented air of the audience chamber would be affected if someone had thrown open a casement for the north wind to blow through.

The King said, "Have you any other sign by which I may know you are sent from God?"

Joan shook her head curtly. "I did not come here to work signs, my Lord. Take me to Orleans. Give me whatever number of men seems to you good. There I will show you signs why I am sent."

Charles nodded. Her answer reassured him. He lifted his hand.

"You have leave to go. Lodging for you, Joan, and for your companions will be provided in the Tower of Coudray. It is a part of this castle. There no harm can come to you." He looked emphatically at the Archbishop. His gaze lingered on Tremouille. When he looked back at the girl, his smile was almost tender. "Be patient only a little longer, Joan." Then he said the thing that she cherished, the thing that she had dreamed of him saying, so that no matter what happened in time to come, her faith in him never faltered, and no man's word could tarnish her bright image of the King. "Joan, I believe in you. I believe that through you, France will be restored. I am not the stuff from which kings are made. Nevertheless, if it is indeed God's will, that I rule the Kingdom of France, I will keep faith with you who bring me this help, as best I can." He spoke with the humility that was habitual to him.

Joan's eyes glistened with tears. She looked at Jean. She looked at Bertrand. She looked back at Charles.

He said to Jean gravely, "I thank you for bringing her to me. I will give her a household of her own, but you will be her special guardians at all times."

Jean felt that the King was speaking of a time that was still in the remote future. He felt that the King was making covenant with them to ride with Joan no matter what happened. He did not know why, for he was not given to dramatic gestures, but suddenly he drew his sword and presented it by the pommel to Charles. He knelt before him, as if they were alone, and not in the presence of the entire Court.

"By my knighthood, I swear it," he said simply. Then he stood up. The King returned his sword. The three of them bowed. Taking Joan by the hand, Jean led her from the audience chamber.

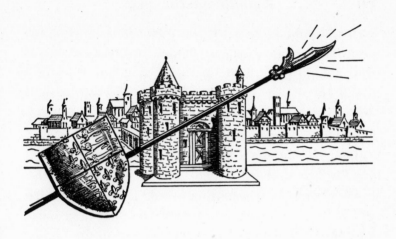

Chapter IV—The City

JEAN STOOD IN THE COURTYARD OF THE HOUSE OF JACQUES
Boucher in Orleans. He held the reins of a great Flemish war horse. The horse was pure white, and the
leather of its saddle and bridle were white, embossed

with silver fleurs-de-lis. Jean rubbed its velvety nose,
while he waited. Upstairs in the house he could hear
Joan calling impatiently for them to hurry for there
was fighting and she was not there. Jean smiled, but
there was no amusement in his smile. Away westward
he could hear the familiar din of battle, the roar of
cannon, the shrieks of the wounded and the war cry of
the English soldiers, which held such terror for the
French. He, too, wished they would hurry. His squire
and Bertrand's stood at a distance holding their mas-
ters' horses, and their heavy battle axes. In the house,
Bertrand was helping Joan into the polished white
armor that together with the great horse had been the
King's parting gift before he sent her to Orleans.

He heard the clatter of steel and the ring of chain
mail on the stairway. Bareheaded, and flushed with
excitement Joan stood in the door. She held a sword
in both hands. Bertrand clattered down behind her,
carrying her banner.

"Jean help me. My fingers tremble so that I cannot
fasten my sword. Of your courtesy, help me."

Looping the bridle of her horse over his arm, he
came up to her. He took the sword from her. He
touched it with the same reverence that he would
have touched the legendary sword of Roland. It was
very old and worn. Five crosses were scratched on the
silver hilt. He remembered the morning in Chinon
when the King told Joan that her troubles were at an

end, that the Church had found her innocent of any evil intention. "Your army stands ready to march," he concluded with a smile at the joy she was unable to contain. She clasped her hands like a child. "And I have provided you with the horse and the armor you will need, Joan. Come down to the courtyard and see for yourself."

In the courtyard two grooms held the magnificent white horse, and the smith who had made the shining armor stood by the great chest in which it had been brought to the castle. They had all smiled at Joan's exclamation of delight. "You will need another sword," Charles had said, glancing at the plain one she wore.

She had looked at him silently for a moment.

"There is a sword for me," she said, "buried beneath the altar in the chapel of Saint Catherine at Fierbois." The King stared. "How do you know, Joan?" he asked gently.

"My lady Catherine told me last night. She told me that I should send for this one. This sword had been used by many good knights, but only to uphold justice or to defend the helpless. My lady Catherine said I should wear it into battle."

At her casual reference to her Saint, the King crossed himself; even Tremouille and the Archbishop who shadowed the King everywhere, felt a chill of superstitious awe touch them.

"I will send for it," Charles said. "Jean de Metz, you

are to ride to Fierbois this very morning. Direct the priests of the chapel to dig for this sword. If they find it, bring it back to Chinon immediately."

Jean had bowed and left the royal presence to arm himself. . . . Somehow, as he rode out of Chinon, he had no doubt the sword would be found, Saint Catherine's sword that had been used only in the cause of justice and mercy. . . .

He buckled the white leather belt about Joan's waist. He made a stirrup of his hands and tossed her lightly up into her saddle.

"My banner," she cried. Bertrand handed her the banner. It was of white fringed silk with the names of the Lord and His Mother embroidered on a field of lilies. The two knights mounted. They fell in on either side of the girl. She spurred the white stallion to a trot.

"Why, oh why did they not wait for me?" She looked from one to the other, as they rode toward the Burgundian gate.

Jean said, "They did not wait, they did not call you because the council of Captains was divided in the matter."

"But Dunois and La Hire are my friends, I know they are my friends. Surely—"

"Joan, you are an untried girl," Bertrand interrupted. "You must prove yourself in battle even as a young knight must prove himself. Beside," he added, teasingly, "being men, they are jealous because you have told them that you will raise the siege of this city of Orleans in less than five days, a thing which they, for all their experience, have not accomplished in the long months they have been here."

"Oh," said Joan, "but I do nothing. It is the King of Heaven who will do it all. I only fulfill His command."

"Joan."

"Yes?"

Jean sighed. Then he began again. "See now, not all men know, as we know that you are sent by God. The English think you a witch. You have enemies at the Court of the King himself. Tremouille and his Grace the Archbishop of Reims were responsible for the decision that wasted so much time, when we brought the army from Blois, and marched them up the wrong side of the river. Dunois thought it might be safer for you that way, he honestly did, but the Archbishop had told him that you were not to be trusted. How was he to know, until he met you?"

Joan roweled the white horse into a canter.

"Surely the Archbishop serves God and the King?" she said doubtfully.

"Perhaps. But it is open knowledge that both he and Tremouille have taken money from the English and the Burgundians, just to keep our Lord the King from sending aid to this city. So be careful, Joan, I beg of you."

She looked at him, a smile indented the corners of her mouth. "You be careful, my friend."

Jean thought it odd that she did not warn Bertrand in the same way, but he was not curious. He did not pursue the matter.

Beyond the Burgundian gate the din of a battle raging fiercely, came to them. As they cantered up, two men brushed past them. Between them they supported a third. From the great femoral artery in his thigh, blood spurted with a terrible rhythm. It splattered the white stallion's forelegs. Joan's eyes grew dark with terror and pity.

"What is it?" she gasped.

"A dying Frenchman," one of the soldiers answered laconically. He did not even glance up at her.

"How goes it with our men yonder?" Jean questioned.

"We have attacked the bastion of Saint Loup. But even Dunois cannot take that. By evening," the laconic voice filled with bitterness, "the English will have it again, and there will be another field of French carrion for the wolves to feast upon."

"No!" The word struck like a lash. Joan spurred her horse so that he reared, squealing with pain. "No, they shall not have it. Open the gate." One of the squires hastened to obey her. Joan galloped through into the field. The green grass of spring was trampled and slippery with the blood of the fallen. The noonday sun had drawn the black May flies to the wounds of the dying. The arrows flew thickly about her unprotected head. High above her the buzzards circled, waiting. Joan saw a fair-haired English lad lift his longbow and take aim. He was near enough so she could see the freckles on his sun-browned cheeks. He looked like her brother Pierre, she thought. Suddenly he flung up his hands clutching his throat. The bow fell as he pitched forward on his face, a French arrow through his jugular vein. Suddenly a white hot anger possessed her. That men should kill each other in hatred, that the stench of their blood and the screams of their agony should despoil the fair green day that the King of Heaven had sent as a gift to both French and English, for surely springtime was the same, she thought, in all the world? Such anger possessed Joan at the waste of it, she brought her free hand down with stinging force on the white stallion's rump.

"Forward," she cried, "forward," and the scattered French saw the great horse leap under her. Dunois galloped to her side, Jean pressing closely on her left. Her silvery armor blazed in the sun. "Boldly!" she cried. "Boldly!" And her cry was the call of a trumpet to the disorganzed army. The archers re-formed at her back. The French horsemen charged as a single unit, and she rode before them at a gallop, her white banner blowing in the spring wind.

The English lines held for a moment, then they

broke, the footmen and horsemen alike stampeding in the direction of safety, with cries of "Sorcery," "Witchcraft." In vain Sir William Glasdale, the English commander, endeavored to hold them. At last he, too, was forced to turn and ride for his life.

The French took with ease the bastion of Saint Loup, which had once been a church.

Joan saw her soldiers drive a miserable group of six English archers from the sanctuary, where they had taken refuge. One of them drew his dagger and plunged it into an Englishman's defenseless back.

"No," she sobbed, "oh, no. Tell them, Dunois, tell them not to kill any more this day." Dunois looked at her in astonishment. But he shouted the order.

Saint Loup was theirs. Tears ran down Joan's face. She tried to smile at Jean, as he pulled a linen kerchief from his girdle. He wiped her face. For a moment, their horses stood close. For a moment he cradled her black head against his shoulder, as she leaned against him. Then she straightened, and wheeled about. They galloped toward the city, from which they could already hear the joyous tolling of bells.

It was dawn. It was the last day. Saint Jean le Blanc had fallen. Les Augustins, the greatest English fortress, had been burned. Les Tourelles only remained. It was dawn, and Joan lay watching the dawn light silver the mist rising from the river. She had been

sleeping on her side, wrapped in Jean's cloak. He slept
at her feet. Dunois and La Hire, her staunch allies
among the captains, slept on either side of her. Bertrand de Poulengy lay just within reach of her hand.
She looked at him with a sorrowful foreboding tenderness. It was dawn, and she knew what would happen,
because her friends had come in the night and they
had warned her.

Catherine had told her, her own young and ardent
voice thickened with tears as she told Joan. "The walls
of this fort are high. You will try to climb one of the
scaling ladders too, so that you can be always with
your men. You will be wounded between your shoulder and your left breast probably. One of your companions will suffer also in this battle."

"Which one?"

"I cannot tell you, Joan."

"Will he die, think you?"

"Do not fear. Our Lord, the King of Heaven will
be with you both."

Joan thought that she would not be afraid when the
moment came. She hoped she wouldn't cry, and dis-
hearten her men. At the thought of being hurt she
winced. She touched the muscle between breast and
shoulder and knew that she was already afraid of the
pain. About her companions, she did not even want to
think; they were both so dear to her, she did not see

how she could get along without them. Then the ab-
solute solitude of her own heart flooded through her
like a great silence, bringing its own strange consolation. The King of Heaven would look after them all.
They were His, and His Compassion was not just for
this silver morning, it was forever.

A trumpet sounded. Another answered it. Church
bells summoned the faithful to Mass in the city beyond
the encampment.

Joan sprang to her feet. She shook the black hair out
of her eyes. She combed it with her fingers. She had
slept in her armor. It remained only to gird on her
sword. One of the squires who had come with her from
Vaucouleurs brought the white stallion; his coat
gleamed with the silver dew of morning.

"Arise, lazy one." Joan nudged Bertrand with her
foot. He sprang up. Jean rolled over grumbling and
got to his feet. Dunois and La Hire rose silently. They
waited. They had grown used to Joan's ways, and all
of them respected her stubbornness in matters of faith.
They had seen the results. A priest, a brother in one
of the humble mendicant orders that roamed the land,
had been chosen by Joan to act as her spiritual guide.
He came to her now, smiling, and the little group fell
on their knees in the dew-drenched field while he began to say his Mass. When they had received the Holy
Sacrament, they drank red wine and devoured thick

black bread. Then they mounted their horses and turned in the direction of the river.

La Hire pulled his grizzled beard. He reined up beside Joan. "The defenses are simple," he said. "At the entrance to the bridge a short distance from Les Augustins there is an embankment and a deep ditch. Behind the embankment you understand, there is the wooden drawbridge that connects it with Les Tourelles. These two great towers must themselves be taken first. Are you sure, Joan, of the counsel you have received in this thing?" His voice was almost gentle. She smiled at him.

"I am sure. I know that the Tourelles are well nigh impregnable. But we are commanded to attack them. Let us ride." She put her horse into a trot. La Hire, Dunois, and Jean followed her. They plunged into the river, and swam their horses in the direction of the squat forbidding towers.

The morning sun was high. It beat mercilessly on the field of battle. The French army having crossed the river attacked the outer fortification. The men threw up scaling ladders. Archers and foot soldiers armed with maces and pikes began to ascend them. Arrows from the dreaded English longbows and bolts from the crossbows of the invaders flew like hail. And always above the twang of the bowstrings and the clash of iron and steel, sounded the shrieks of anguish as men fell, wounded or slain. . . .

Joan stood with one foot on the bottom rung of a scaling ladder, directing the attack. Beside her Jean stood with drawn sword, to defend her in case of need. Bertrand stood on the ladder, three rungs above her. He was laughing with excitement.

"Did you ever see the like?" he called to Jean. "One could hold the Tourelles forever, with a handful of men. But these English, they are no longer men. Our Maid has turned them into a pack of frightened sheep. The fort will be ours with the going down of this day's sun."

Suddenly a crossbowman appeared at the top of the ladder. He took deliberate aim with his unwieldy, murderous weapon. The bolt whizzed past Bertrand, even as he threw himself defensively between Joan and the enemy. But he was too late. A strangled cry from the girl as she fell backward into Jean's outstretched arms, warned him that he was too late. He saw the shaft of the bolt half-buried just below her left shoulder. With a yell of rage he sprang up the ladder. He caught the crossbowman by the throat. For a moment they wrestled and swayed on the perilous foothold locked in mortal combat. The bowman flung his weapon from him. He slipped one hand into Bertrand's armpit. In it there, he held a Spanish dagger no more than a palm's breadth in size. He drove it home with such force that Bertrand shrieked once. Then he fell.

At the foot of the ladder all was confusion. Dunois, La Hire, and all Joan's faithful attendants were begging her to let herself be carried from the field of battle.

Jean supported her head against his knee. He took a small silver brandy flask from the pouch at his girdle. He forced it against her pale lips.

"Drink," he ordered harshly. "For I must pull the bolt at once. There may be poison."

Joan swallowed the fiery stuff. She choked and hiccoughed as it burnt her throat and stomach. Between sobs she looked wildly about. "Jean, where is Bertrand? He was above me on the ladder. Oh, no, please, no."

Jean removed her breastplate and gorget. He drove the point of his own dagger with the crude deadly efficiency that years of warfare had taught him, into the girl's flesh, just where the bolt protruded. Dunois and La Hire held her arms behind her back so that she could not struggle.

"No, no," she screamed. Jean paid her no heed. He brought his knife up widening the incision so that he could pull out the deeply imbedded barb. The blood spurted over his hands. For a second he paused.

"Joan," he said. "You must hold still, Joan. Or I will take your life in trying to save it." She looked up at him, her eyes dark with terror and pain. She tensed herself obediently. He went back to work. Suddenly his knife clinked against the bolthead. Gingerly he withdrew it. He rolled his linen kerchief into a ball and plugged the gaping wound. Dunois released her arm. He unwound a blue silk scarf from his breast and shoulders. He passed it to Jean who bandaged it tightly about Joan's own shoulder and breast, knotting the fringed ends about her neck in a sling to support her arm. La Hire pressed the brandy flask to her mouth again.

"Drink." She drank. He forced her to swallow the burning liquor until the color surged up in her chalk-white face.

"Bertrand?" She gasped.

"He fell into the ditch, Joan."

"Is he wounded?"

"He is dead, ma mie. The crossbowman who wounded you carried one of those little Spanish daggers. I saw him use it, even as you fell."

"Oh, Jean!" She looked at him stricken. She forgot her own pain. Suddenly her face twisted and she put it down on her knees and wept like a child.

"It was the way he wanted it, Joan. He was fighting for something he believed in. And it did not hurt. It was quick."

"But I loved him," she sobbed.

"He was my brother, Joan." She looked up at his tense serious face. She saw the white line of pain about his mouth. His dark eyes were wet. She put out her good hand and he grasped it strongly.

"I did not know it would be like this," she said.

"Did you know?"

"Oh yes, they told me. My lady Catherine told me in the night. That I would be wounded and that"—she choked back another sob—"that one of my companions would suffer. I did not know which one. But our Lord, the King of Heaven, will take care of Bertrand. I knew," she repeated brokenly, "but I did not know it would be like this. Oh Jean, I didn't."

"Will you let us carry you from the field, Joan? It goes hard with our men. Perhaps tomorrow we should try but now . . . ?" Dunois interrupted gently.

"No!" Joan shook her head. "No, I beg of you. Dunois, La Hire! Lift me up. Put me on my horse." Reluctantly La Hire commanded the white stallion brought to the edge of the embankment. Jean lifted her into her saddle.

"He was fighting for something he believed in," she whispered vehemently as he lifted her. "And I am fighting for the thing he believed in. I am sorry I cried. Forgive me, Jean." He could not speak. He touched the hilt of her sword. She smiled down at him with profound tenderness, her face lighted with a passionate secret exaltation.

Then she stood up in her stirrups. "Now," she cried,

"now, forward!" The French saw her lift the white banner high. With a great shout of triumph they hurled themselves at the scaling ladders.

It would be as Joan said it would be. Before the going down of the sun the Tourelles would be theirs. Orleans would be free.

Chapter V—The Crown

JOAN KNOCKED TIMIDLY. JEAN DE METZ STOOD BESIDE her, holding the white silk banner. The royal guards stationed at either side of the great double doors behind which could be heard the steady ebb and flow of voices, looked at her with ill-concealed curiosity.

The July sunlight streamed over the girl in her battered silver armor. She felt hot, but the palms of her hands were damp. She knocked again.

"Enter."

The guards moved forward. They opened the doors of the council hall with deliberate ceremonial care. In the tapestried chamber, on an oak bench with a mantle of crimson velvet about his shoulders, sat the King.

Tremouille and the Archbishop were with him. As Joan crossed the room to throw herself on her knees before Charles, they turned their backs. The atmosphere was thick with their unspoken antagonism. Jean stopped at the threshold. He bowed low to the King.

"My Lord, much of my work is done," Joan said abruptly. "There is little time to spare and no time at all to waste, if I am to finish it indeed, as I was commanded to do."

"But Joan," the King would have lifted her to her feet, but she knelt stubbornly in front of him.

"Up and down the Loire the cities have been delivered from their English and Burgundian enemies. Everywhere in France the people clamor only for their King. My Lord, must you be forever in council? Are not deeds better than words? Surely now the time is ripe. Come with me to Reims. Receive the crown of your fathers. It is for this I was sent, my Lord. You know, for I told you at Chinon when Jean de Metz brought me to you."

Charles flinched. "I know, Joan," he said wearily, "but His Grace, the Archbishop and the Sire de la Tremouille, they are my chief advisers. And they counsel delay."

"Wherefore?"

The question was unexpected. It startled the Archbishop and Tremouille. They turned to stare at the peasant girl who presumed to question a king. It startled Charles too but as always, when she came to him, he felt stronger, and quite suddenly capable of making decisions.

"Wherefore, indeed?" he repeated. "You have won back three quarters of a kingdom for the crown of France, and I, its unworthy King, am slow to accept so great a gift.

"Joan," he said, "I will come to Reims with you. I will start in three days' time. I will be crowned with the crown of France, and anointed with the holy oil of Saint Remy on the seventeenth of July. Will that suffice?"

Joan smiled up at him through a mist of happy tears.

"Oh yes, my Lord," she breathed, "oh, yes."

The Archbishop looked at her. Jean, glancing at him, saw death in his face. But he did no more than bow as Charles turned to him for confirmation.

"That gives ample time in which to prepare, Your Grace, does it not?"

"Ample time, my Lord," the Archbishop said quietly.

"Then it is an established thing and will surely come to pass as I have said. Tremouille, prepare an edict to be proclaimed in all the loyal cities. Joan, let your heart be at rest. You have leave to go."

He lifted her to her feet. She stooped and kissed his hand in her gratitude. Then she followed Jean from the council chamber.

Morning gilded the spires of Reims Cathedral. The sun burned through the clouds on the eastern horizon, flooding the entire city with golden light. Presently crowds began to filter into the cathedral square, until it was one mass of seething humanity.

Jean stood in the cool dimness of the sanctuary, and watched as the great central doors were flung wide.

Charles of Valois waited by the high altar. He wore a somber gown of black velvet, slashed at neck and elbow to show his cloth of gold tunic. Joan stood at the foot of the sanctuary steps. She held her banner staff so tightly her knuckles were white against the brown flesh. She wore her silver armor, and over it a white silk jupon embroidered with the lilies of France, the gift of the King. Her unruly black hair was plastered slick and shining on her forehead. It was newly washed and trimmed by the court barber. Her brown, wind-burned face, freckled and peeling from the sun, was rapt in a strange beauty.

The trumpets sounded. The music of their summons echoed and re-echoed in the vaulted silence of the cathedral. The Archbishop who stood at the King's left stepped past him, while through the door walked four peers of the realm, leading a milk-white horse by the bits. On the horse's back sat the abbot of Saint Remy. In his trembling blue-veined hands he carried the golden reliquary shaped like a dove in which the holy oil was kept. The Duc d'Alençon and the Sire de Rais lifted the old man from his saddle. A page led the white horse away. Again the trumpets sounded their great golden music, while the Archbishop anointed Charles king in deed and in truth. One of the Dukes stepped forward. He buckled the sword of state about the King's waist. Then the King knelt at the Archbishop's feet, and the crown was placed on his head. The Archbishop's hands held his in the ancient gesture of homage, while Charles swore to defend the Faith, to rule with justice and mercy, and go humbly with his God.

As he stood up and turned to face the people, the Abbot of Saint Remy flung the ermine bordered mantle of purple velvet over his shoulders.

Charles looked at the girl. He, like Jean, was struck by the rapt beauty of her face. Something passed between them in that look. Then she forgot the people, she forgot the holy rite. She flung herself at his feet and embraced his knees.

"My Lord," she whispered, "now at last it is finished. Now at last I have done what the King of Heaven commanded me to do. All the world knows you now for the rightful King of France."

"Without you this day would never have dawned," he returned gently. "Come, I wish the people to know my gratitude to you and your Master the King of Heaven."

Then to the amazement of everyone, he took her by the hand and led her down the aisle that was carpeted in scarlet velvet. Out he led her into the golden flooding sunlight. Behind them the cathedral choir burst into the mighty "Te deum" of a nation's thanksgiving. Behind them the Archbishop stood: his cold venomous eyes met the eyes of Tremouille who stood in shadow by the chancel rail.

"But my Lord," said Tremouille in his chill, reasonable voice, "Joan is a young girl carried away by the victories she shared and your coronation at which she was honored, as no man in the history of France has been honored."

Charles shrugged irritably. He stood at the window of the council chamber in the castle at Soissons. Outside a summer rain fell in torrents. He was cold and miserable. He was sick of argument. He wished Tremouille and the Archbishop would leave him in peace. He was fully prepared to ride from Reims to Paris with

Joan and the victorious army the day after his coronation, swept as he was by the high emotion of that moment. But in the night, his two councilors visited him.
His indecisive nature did the rest.

He idled in Reims until Thursday of the week following. Then at Tremouille's instigation, commanding
Joan to follow, he took the Court to Soissons. Now,
cold and miserable, he wished he had fulfilled Joan's
request. They might have been in Paris but for Tremouille, he thought, and wondered with weary irony
what his treacherous councilors stood to gain from the
delay. The trouble is, he thought, I don't care. I know
that they are greedy and treacherous but I don't care.
All I wish is peace. Tremouille has run the kingdom,
and I have been left in peace to dream away my life.
This is how it has been always. This is how I wish it
to be. His lip curled faintly in self-contempt. He
turned wearily back to his chief councilor.

"What would you? For three days I have heard
nothing but your lies and insinuations about Joan. She
wanted to take Paris. Paris is the capital of France. It
was poorly defended and the road lay open to us.
Without Paris I am but half a King. Now the English
have sent reinforcements into the city to the number
of five thousand, and you prattle to me about the wis-
dom of delay! That girl knows more of warfare than
you and de Chartres together will ever know."

Tremouille waited patiently. He was used to such tirades.

Someone knocked on the door. "Enter," Charles said petulantly. The Archbishop swept in, his velvet robes rustling softly.

"I bring good tidings, my Lord. All France will rejoice when they are published."

"Well?"

"Burgundy wishes to make peace. The Duke has sent me this treaty to lay before you. If the terms seem to you good, there will be peace in France before the year is out."

"But Paris is still in enemy hands!"

"True, my Lord, but the English together with the Burgundians will render the city into your possession in fifteen days' time. It is so written here. Only you must declare a truce. Joan and her captains must not be allowed to march on Paris, or on any other city."

"It would indeed bring peace, my Lord," Tremouille said, "and the land is in greater need of peace than of seventeen-year-old maidens who declare themselves sent of God." He had gone too far.

Charles's face whitened in sudden fury. "And where would you be, bloodsucking leech, if we had not listended to this maiden? She promised to restore the kingdom and crown me King. These things she has done. If a quarter of the kingdom is still in enemy hands, the fault does not lie with Joan. It lies with me, inasmuch as I have listened to your counsel rather than hers."

"My Lord," the Archbishop began soothingly. But Charles, roused at last from his dreaming, would not listen. He clapped his hands sharply. A page entered through the great door.

"Bring hither the maid Joan at once." The page bowed, and glided silently out.

"My Lord," the Archbishop's tone was urgent. "Before you admit her, we must tell you something. In this treaty, the English offer a price for Joan. They think she is a witch. They think her victories come not of God but of Satan who has taught her the witchcraft she practices. They, if they can lay hands on her would have her examined by the Holy Inquisition and then burned at the stake."

The King shuddered.

"Think, my Lord, the price of one life for the lives of so many Frenchmen. Give Joan to them and both Burgundians and English will withdraw from the towns they hold. Paris will be yours without further bloodshed. It will bring peace, such peace as the realm has not known in a hundred years."

He hammered at Charles. The King looked at him contemptuously.

"Before God, I am not such a one. She came to me

in good faith, and in good faith I pledged her my help. Would you have me sell her to the English after what she has done for me?"

"For the sake of peace, my Lord, for the sake of peace in France," the Archbishop said softly, "you would give much, for you are its King."

Tremouille looked at him pityingly. "It is possible, my Lord, that you were deceived in the girl. Many bishops and doctors of the Church think that you were deceived from the beginning. There is no need to give her to the English anyway. But for the sake of peace—" He looked away from Charles. They had him where they wanted him at last, and they knew it. Charles struggled with himself. He was a loyal son of Holy Church. He wanted nothing to do with witchcraft. If learned doctors of the Church thought Joan was not come from God, perhaps after all Tremouille was right. . . . His head ached with the effort to make a decision. And peace, peace at any price was better than this endless bickering. And if the treaty said they would give him Paris in fifteen days' time . . . He looked beseechingly at the Archbishop. He looked beseechingly at Tremouille. "Help me," he begged. "Advise me in this matter."

"There is no need to give Joan to the English," Tremouille repeated. "Only sign the treaty, and when Joan comes here, refuse her permission to make further war on the English or on the Burgundians. If she flouts your royal authority, or if any of the army flouts it by following her standard into battle, you are blameless, my Lord, should she indeed fall into their hands."

Charles nodded listlessly. As usual Tremouille had found a way out for him. The Archbishop picked up a quill. He dipped it into the black inkpot that stood on the council table.

"Sign, my Lord," he urged. He laid the treaty parchment in front of the King. "Sign." There was a hesitant knock on the door. Almost guiltily Charles slashed his signature across the document. "Enter," he said curtly. Joan stood on the threshold, Jean de Metz beside her.

"You sent for me, my Lord?" she said eagerly. The King was silent. Joan looked from Tremouille to the Archbishop. Apprehension flooded her being.

"What is it, oh, what is it?"

Charles felt the first stab of guilt. He said sullenly, "Can you read, Joan?"

"No, my Lord," she said in astonishment.

He shoved the document he had signed toward her. She could not read, but she recognized the great seals of Burgundy and England attached to the parchment. And she recognized the King's scrawling signature. Her shoulders tensed. "What is it, my Lord?"

"I have signed a treaty with Burgundy. The terms

are favorable. In fifteen days they will yield me Paris. But the treaty demands a military truce. You must not violate this part of it. If you fight or if any of your men fight with the English or their allies of Burgundy I will disown you. For you will have disobeyed my royal command!"

"My Lord!" Joan looked at him stricken. "My Lord, surely you cannot mean this!"

Charles looked at her white face. For a moment he considered tearing the parchment in two. Then the guilt stabbed him, and he grew angry. Would they never leave him in peace, the girl who spoke as truthfully to him as his own conscience, or the councilors who offered him a solution to the problems of conscience that was both wise and easy? Sullenly he spoke, "Surely I mean it. You are not to ride forth to war."

"But this treaty is a lie," Joan exploded. "All they want is to gain time, while they build up their reserves and defenses. Oh believe me, my Lord." She threw herself on her knees as she had so long ago at Chinon. "Believe me, they wish only to trick you. I am a stupid girl, but this much is plain to me!" She spoke with such passionate conviction, Charles was moved from anger to pity despite himself. He glanced hesitatingly at Tremouille. Jean saw Tremouille shake his head. Briefly. Emphatically. She saw the gesture. And sud-

denly she understood. She had indeed been tricked.
She had been betrayed. Somehow both she and Jean
recognized the King's agony of indecision, and recognized how little he understood the thing he had done.

"You have leave to go," the King said preemptorily.

Joan blinked back the tears. For the last time Jean
took her by the hand, and bowing as he did so, led her
from the King's presence.

At the door he turned and looked once at Charles.
Better than Joan he comprehended the dangers into
which the King's unwitting treachery would throw her.
In that look Charles saw his desire for peace, his desire
to escape the responsibilities of his calling, mirrored
back for what they were. He said harshly to the Archbishop and Tremouille. "You also have leave to go."
In bewilderment they bowed and left him alone.

Alone, Charles sat down on an oaken settle. He sat
with his hands hanging heavily between his knees. If
they capture her, he thought, if they burn her, as Tremouille said, I am responsible. The thought sent a
twinge of remorse through him, because he knew he
had loved Joan as much as he could ever love anyone.
Then he thought again, they will burn her, and I will
be responsible. He bowed his head upon his knees and
wept, not for his own treachery, not for the knowledge
that in the end she would be captured, fighting for him
and for his kingdom. He wept because his heart was

stone within him. He did not care. For his treachery, for her capture, for the kingdom itself, he did not care. So that they left him in peace, he did not care. And knowing these things of himself, he wept bitterly.

Chapter VI — The Captive

JOAN WENT FROM THE KING TO THE TOP OF THE WATCH-
tower of Soissons. The rain fell in slanting icy sheets,
blown by the cutting east wind. She lifted her face to
the storm-dark sky. One hand clenched round the hilt
of her sword. With the other she held to the stone ram-
part. Heedless of her drenched tunic and wet hair, she
gazed desperately into the unresponsive clouds. Tears
ran down her face. They were salt in her mouth.

"Why is it like this, oh why?" she moaned.

She felt something warm and comforting flung across her shoulders. Without turning her head, she knew that Jean had climbed the tower stairs after her, and the warmth was his cloak, with which he had shielded her so many times. She felt absurdly comforted by its warmth, so that the hard knot of despair in her chest dissolved in a hot flood of tears. He waited. When she could weep no more, he said, "Joan, you knew this might come to pass, for you were warned."

"I know," she said wearily, "but for a moment it seemed to me that all the King of Heaven bade me do would be undone by this treaty."

"No, Joan, to drive the last English invader from our land may take longer without you, but I believe it will be accomplished. You have roused all of us from our despair. We will fight now, because you have given us something to believe in. Something to hope for. Freedom."

She gazed at him wistfully. "And a man will fight for something he believes in," she repeated.

"Yes, Joan. Will you come down now, out of the wind and the storm?"

She nodded.

"And there is something else. Count John of Luxembourg is encamped before Compiegne with a Burgundian army. The people of Compiegne are in sore distress. They have begged the King that you be sent

to them. The messenger told us about it in the castle
hall at the morning bread."

"Why did the King not tell me?"

"Because, Joan, Tremouille and the Archbishop had
persuaded him to sign the treaty with Burgundy. They
do not want to see the English driven out. The English
together with the Burgundians have doubtless paid
them a high price in gold, to see that Charles our
King signed that worthless paper."

At the bitterness in his voice, Joan laid her hand on
his arm.

"But the treaty is nothing. They say they will give
Paris to the King if I go not forth to battle again. I
do not believe this. They wish only to gain time.
And—" she finished desperately, "what will happen
to the poor people of Compiegne?"

"We shall collect such of the men as will follow you.
The treaty is not yet ratified, ma mie. You cannot be
said to have flouted the authority of your King until it
has been carried back to the Duke of Burgundy himself. Do you understand? The captains, Dunois because of the royal blood in his veins, La Hire because
he is a commander in chief cannot go with you. But
you, you who have no title and no position to maintain,
you may go. The King," he said with brutal candor,
"will probably be relieved to see you go. You have
embarrassed him."

Joan's mouth trembled.

"Do not cry any more. The men will follow you, and the miserable people of Compiègne will welcome you. They need your help."

Joan laughed suddenly and joyously. She seized him by the hand and dragged him toward the stairs.

"Let us hurry then. We will ride to Compiegne. And when our Lord the King has seen how the enemy fall before us, perhaps he will destroy this treaty." She pushed the wet black fringe of hair off her forehead, and tucked the wind-blown strands behind her ears. Jean smiled at the transformation. He reached for the iron handle of the tower door to open it for her.

"Joan," he said, "Joan."

She was beside him still, but he realized with terror that she had not heard him. She stood beside him, her face drained of color, her eyes dark as she gazed through him and beyond him. She was beside him, but her spirit was not with him. It had fled in answer to another summons, as surely as it fled that starry night in the forest when he had lain sleepless while she prayed. He let go the handle of the door. He would have left her, but he feared that she might fall on the roughly hewn stone of the staircase. She smiled that radiant smile he had come to know, and she reached out with such spontaneous joy, he thought for a moment that he was seeing the thing that she was seeing.

Then she knelt. When she spoke, her voice lilted with the joy that was in her.

"My lady Margaret! My lady Catherine. You came. I needed you so, and you came!" She sank back on her heels, hands clasped tight like those of a child just learning to say its prayers. She listened. The smile faded. The dark gray eyes grew frightened. Then her back tensed. The color flushed her white face with life. She sighed. She nodded her head.

"Before Saint John's day? I am frightened, but I will try to be of good cheer." She nodded with grave acquiescence.

"Will you come to me then?" She smiled. Watching her, Jean knelt and crossed himself, for that smile mirrored what Joan beheld in all its compassion and its unearthly radiant beauty. The rain spattered her face, and the wind blew the hair back from her forehead, making her look young and awkward and vulnerable.

Suddenly she got to her feet. She waited quietly for a moment. Jean stood up.

"I will be captured before Saint John's day," she said simply. "It is to be. They have told me."

"We will not go to Compiegne," Jean said decisively. But she shook her head, still smiling.

"We will go, my friend. I will be captured somewhere. They did not tell me the place. They only told me I would be captured and that the King of Heaven would take care of me. Would it not be better to go and help people who are already in sore trouble, rather than to skulk about this castle where I am of no use to anyone? My lady Margaret and my lady Catherine have never deceived me. If I am indeed to be captured, then it seems to me of no consequence where I am caught."

Jean leaned forward and kissed her gently on the forehead.

"Come then," he said, and held wide the tower door.

There was a bridge. There was a moat filled with stagnant green water. There was sun—a white blazing sun, that made their heavy armor almost unbearable. The horses foamed at the mouth, blood and foam ran down their sides from the jabbing spurs.

Men and horses reeked of sweat and blood and the green meadow beyond the bridge resounded with the shrieks of the wounded and the dying. Above the bridge and the green water and the fighting, the town and fortress of Compiègne brooded peacefully.

Jean lifted his battle-ax and struck viciously at a Burgundian archer who had seized the bridle of Joan's horse.

"Come," he shouted, "come. We are surrounded. If we do not make haste, they will be forced to close the gate of the town and leave us without." She turned on him.

"Be still. It is with us to help the town. It is with us

to defeat their enemies. Fight, Jean, fight." He wheeled his horse. The sword flashed in a shining arc over his head. He heard a man scream as he fell, and suddenly as one possessed he drove his spurs home in the stallion's bleeding flanks, and sent him at a racing gallop straight into a cluster of Burgundian knights among whom he recognized John, Count of Luxembourg. Behind him, Joan cried out. He saw Count John raise the terrible English mace, but he could not check the pain-maddened stallion in time to parry the blow. It shattered his sword like glass, then a million suns wheeled through the sky and he felt himself falling, falling through a fathomless dark.

Jean stared up at the white ceiling. It was rough, the stone was veined with age. He realized suddenly that it was white because the sun was shining. He looked down and saw that he lay on a wooden couch like a trestle. A white wool coverlet slid to the floor as he moved, and an excruciating pain shot through his head.

"No, no now, you must lie still."

"Where am I, what place is this?" he demanded.

"You are in the Dominican priory, at Compiègne."

"Compiegne? But how came I here?"

"There was a battle, my son," the voice said patiently. "Surely you remember the battle? They said you fought like one gone mad. You were struck down by Count John of Luxembourg himself. It was he who took Joan, the Maid of Lorraine prisoner."

"Joan? What happened to her?" he cried. "What happened?" He tried to see his informant but when he lifted his head, the terrible pain shot through it again. Sensing what he wanted, the speaker came to the side of his couch. He wore the cowled black and white habit of Saint Dominic.

"She was taken to Rouen."

"What have they done to her?"

"She is the prisoner of the English. They have paid Count John ten thousand livres for possession of the girl. She is in an English prison. But she is on trial for heresy and witchcraft before a Court of the Holy Inquisition."

"She is no witch!"

The monk threw back his hood. His face was old and gentle. There were laughter lines carved deep around his eyes and his mouth.

"No," he said, "I do not think she is a witch. But the English do. And Pierre Cauchon, the Bishop of Beauvais, it is he who sits in judgment on the girl's case. He thinks she is a witch."

Jean closed his eyes. Tears, the tears of his bodily weakness ran down his white cheeks.

"You make a woman of me," he murmured.

"You have been nigh death from the wound in your head, my son."

"Has it been a long time since the battle?"

"Yes, it has been months since Compiegne fell again into English hands."

"Am I not then a prisoner?"

"No. Our sympathies were with the rightful King, Charles. We had besought his help against Burgundy. He did not send it, as you are well aware. But Joan came, with such men as would follow her. That is how you came here. Do you remember any of it, my son?"

He remembered that long, long ago, he had pledged his knightly word to a girl dressed in a man's tunic and wearing a man's sword, that he would be with her whatever happened. He had to go to her somehow. But the monk was speaking.

"Our sympathies were with the King, so when the battle was over, some of the townspeople went down into the meadow to bury the slain. I went with some of my priests that they might have Christian burial. We waited until night for it was a dangerous thing to do. You had been left on the field for dead. But you still breathed so we carried you up here."

"I am grateful. My name is Jean de Metz."

"I am the Superior of this House," the old man said. "I know your name because in your fever wanderings, you spoke often of yourself and a certain Bertrand de

Poulengy. It was you then, who carried Joan to Chinon in the first place?"

"Yes." He saw the ring on the Abbot's finger. He saw the black and white habit, and it took on a sudden fearful significance in his weary brain.

"But you priests of Saint Dominic are the priests of the Holy Inquisition. It is before such as you that Joan is on trial. If she is found guilty of heresy and witchcraft, the Inquisition will give her back to the English, and they will burn her."

The Abbot nodded gravely.

"But you have tended me," he cried.

"Yes."

"What of the King? Does he not care? Has he not tried to ransom her?"

"He does not care."

"Lord Abbot, help me. I must go to Rouen."

"The city is in English hands."

"I cannot help it. I must go to Joan. I promised her I would be with her whatever happened. Will you help me to go to Rouen?"

"I will help you, my son. As soon as you are strong enough to travel you shall go. I will tell you why I do this. I am a very old man. Soon I shall be accounting before my God for the service I have rendered or not rendered to His children on earth. I think Joan will be found guilty. I think she will die. But she will not die because she has trafficked with the Powers of Evil. She will die because Pierre Cauchon is a wicked servant of Holy Church. I know that the English have promised him an Archbishopric and a great barony if he can force the court to find Joan guilty. There will be some priests of Saint Dominic who sincerely believe that Cauchon is right. Perhaps they are English. Or perhaps their sympathies lie with the English cause. I know not. But I will help you journey to Rouen, which is the only way in which I can help Joan. So that I may not stand accused before my God of having neglected even the least of these, His little ones."

Jean said nothing. His dark eyes were fixed gratefully on the old man's face. After a little the Abbot continued.

"One of my young priests, Father Massieu, is constantly with Joan. He was trained here, but he is under obedience to Bishop Cauchon because he was transferred to Rouen four years ago. He has been rebuked more than once for trying to help Joan at the trial. He has written to me, and that is how I know what is intended for her."

Jean waited. "I will give you the habit of Saint Dominic. We will tonsure your head, and give you a safe conduct. As a priest attached to the Inquisition, and bearing a letter from me to Father Massieu, your presence in Rouen will go unquestioned. If he thinks it expedient for you to see the girl, he will arrange it. That is all. Now you must sleep, my son. You will need your strength." The Abbot rose. He made the sign of the Cross on Jean's forehead. Then he left the cell.

Jean stared up at the dappling sunlight on the wall. A north wind blew through the cloister rich with the quickening promise of spring.

Jean stared at the golden sunlight. He thought how lonely she must be. He hoped that she had a window in her prison. He hoped she could see the sun. He turned his face to the wall and wept.

Chapter VII—The Victory

JOAN SAT UPON HER BENCH. SHE FELT THE DAWN COME. She had learned the hour of its coming because the dank air in her cell grew colder. Water dripped endlessly from the stone ceiling above her head. She pulled her feet out of the wet straw that covered the planking. She pulled her knees up. She hugged them clenching her hands tightly together for warmth. She thought the stench of the filthy straw with the constant rustling of the roaches and the rats who inhabited the cell with her was like the stench of a filthy barn that belonged to a peasant in her native village. "Mother," she whispered. "Mother," but it was only a word. She was too cold. She was too tired to remember pain. She was too tired to wince even when the pain of the iron girdle about her waist scraped the raw flesh beneath her filthy tunic as she moved.

She heard the bolt screech on the great door that opened on the corridor connecting her prison with the castle. Her hunched shoulders tensed. She lifted her head, shaking the black fringe out of her eyes. The English guard called to her.

"Arise now." He carried a smoking torch in one hand. In its fitful light, she saw Father Massieu. Obediently she swung her feet over the side of her bench and waited for them to come to her. She could not rise. The chain that shackled her to the post prevented it. As the guard loosed her, the priest put a trembling hand on her head. She felt the mute tenderness of his touch, and it sent a shiver of pure terror through her body.

"Joan," he said. "Joan, I am sent to conduct you to the place where—"

"Where I am to die?" she breathed.

"No, Joan, where you will hear the judgment pronounced. The Bishop would have me bring you to the Cemetery of Saint-Ouen."

She stumbled a little as she followed the priest. The guard walked close behind her. Two more joined him in the corridor.

Joan said, "Is it indeed the month of May?"

"Yes. All the world is spring."

The guards opened a small door cut in the thickness of the wall, and ushered her down a circular staircase into the courtyard. A wooden cart with two solid wheels, drawn by a gray mule waited there. Joan looked at the mule. She looked up at the wind-driven clouds. She looked back at the mule. She thought he was like a gray mule her father owned when she was a child. She wanted to rub the bony convex forehead, and see his long ears flap with pleasure. She wanted to feel the sun-warmed roughness of his skin.

She looked at the black cowl and white robe of the Dominican priest at her side. For a heartbeat he was of the dream and the mule was part of reality. Without thinking, she stepped toward the mule. She touched his forehead. It was warm from the sun.

"Joan," Father Massieu said. The guard seized her roughly from behind. "Mount into the cart, Joan," the priest commanded. He tried to help her, because she stumbled, and would have fallen when her foot touched the step of the cart, but she did not see him. The tears were running down her grimy face, making channels in the grime. Another hand reached from the cart—steadied her roughly. She looked up, and knew by the black clothes he wore that she was looking at Thirache, the executioner of Rouen.

"I wanted to pat the mule," she said. Father Massieu thought she was lightheaded with hunger and fatigue.

Thirache looked at her with pity.

"I know," he said, and slapped the reins on the mule's back. The guards fell in behind them.

In the Cemetery of Saint-Ouen, directly behind the church, there was a great cleared area, where stages were erected in the Christmas season for the performance of miracle plays.

Two stages had been set up during the night. On the larger of the two sat the Bishop, the Vice-Inquisitor, and the rest of the hierarchy of the Church that had come to pronounce judgment on the girl from Lorraine.

On the smaller stage a sour-faced priest waited. He brandished a great sheaf of papers in one hand.

The narrow, crooked streets of Rouen were deserted. The Cemetery of Saint-Ouen was packed with humanity, shouting, cursing humanity, everyone pushing in order to have a glimpse of the Maid.

Thirache plied his whip savagely right and left until the crowd divided and permitted him to drive his cart up to the smaller stage. He did not wait for Joan to dismount this time. He turned and lifted her in his arms. He tossed her up, as he might toss a sack of meal, so that she tumbled at the feet of Guillaume Erard. He drew his robe back in distaste from the touch of her hand, as she tried to right herself. Father Massieu climbed to the stage. He helped her turn so that she faced the stage opposite.

"Make your reverence, Joan," he said gently.

She bowed to Cauchon and the others. They swam before her eyes in a blur of scarlet and gold and green and sapphire. She thought she must have been there before, because she vaguely remembered another place and another time when a blur of scarlet and gold and green had swum before her gaze. Then like the thrust of a sword through the fabric of her dream, she remembered the warm hand of Jean de Metz as it closed over hers when she stood on the threshold of the King's audience chamber in Chinon.

"Jean," she whispered. "Jean." She stared wildly about her, her eyes wide with panic like the eyes of a hunted deer. No warm hand closed over hers. The cold gentle fingers of Father Massieu turned her to face Guillaume Erard. She saw by his robes that he too was a priest and she pulled the black fringe of hair on her forehead as she bent to him.

Then she remembered. Chinon. The King. Orleans. "Jean," she said, "Jean." And knew with sudden dread-

ful clarity that Jean was not with her. That she was
here because she had been captured by the Count of
Luxembourg and sold to the English. That Jean was
not with her and that Catherine had said to her long
ago that it would be like this. When the night was dark
about her, when there was not one star above her,
when it was like this, she must remember that she
would have help. That she would be delivered. "But
where are you?" she sobbed. "Oh where are you, my
lady Catherine?"

Father Massieu tightened his grip on her arm. "You
must be quiet, Joan. You must listen carefully."

Guillaume Erard began to speak in Latin. Fre-
quently he paused, so that Father Massieu could make
his words over into French for the girl.

"The so-called King of France Charles VII is a her-
etic, and he led true Frenchmen from the path of their
duty to God and to France."

Joan shook her head with sudden passion. "My King
is not such a one. He loves France. He loves our Christian faith. He is not such a one as you say."

"Joan, you must listen quietly." Father Massieu
plucked at the ragged sleeve of her tunic.

Erard stepped nearer to where she stood. "Listen,
Joan," his nasal voice was tender. "Listen to me. Submit to the Church. Save your soul. Submit, that is all
we want."

She looked at him. Her gray eyes still reflected panic, but they were luminous with the memory of that other time, that night in the forest when they had been with her, Saint Margaret and Saint Catherine. When they had told her it would be like this. And Jean had been there too, sleeping close against her side, so that she would be warm. . . .

"No one is responsible," she said, her voice shaking. She looked at the sea of angry faces below the stage. The panic held her like a vice.

"If there is fault, it is mine, only mine," she whispered.

Erard touched her hand. "Listen, Joan, listen. You lied about your visions. You lied, I tell you. Retract these things. Retract them now."

"What does it mean—retract?"

"It means that you will sign this paper. It is written here that you lied about your visions, that everything you have done was evil. Retract now or burn!"

"Burn? Retract?" She shook her head wearily as if it were beyond her comprehension.

"Retract or burn," he repeated angrily. Like a chant the crowd took up his words. The sound rose, it swelled in volume. It engulfed her. "Retract, retract." "Burn her, burn her," someone screamed, and suddenly she understood. She looked wildly around. Burn, burn with fire. Retract. Burn.

"No," she sobbed, "no, do not burn me. I will retract. I will do what you want. Do not burn me."

Erard forced a quill into her hand. With trembling fingers, she traced her mark upon the parchment he held.

"Burn her, burn her," screamed the woman's voice, and the crowd took up her words. Someone hurled a stone at the platform. Stones clattered about her like hail.

Thirache lifted her down into the cart. Plying his whip again, he forced the mob to open its ranks and let him through.

Joan lay at his feet, sobbing bitterly. Father Massieu walked beside the mule. As they came to the gate of the cemetery, Joan suddenly heard her name called. She lifted her head. She tried to raise herself. One hand gripped the side of the cart. A hand closed over hers, briefly, warmly.

"Joan, I am here." She looked up, straight into the the dark eyes of Jean de Metz. He stood on the edge of the surging crowd. He was disguised as a Dominican monk. His head was tonsured, and that made him look strange to her. But that protected him from the crowd as effectively as the white habit of the Order. In the confusion and the shouting, no one but Thirache could have been near enough to heed his words.

"I understand, ma mie. It was too much. But I am here."

Thirache pushed her down into the bottom of the cart as a stone struck the mule in the ribs. He lashed at the crowd with his whip.

"Stand aside, monk," he shouted, "unless you would be flogged, too." Jean stepped back quietly. He melted into the throng. But Joan had seen the compassion in his face, and she knew now what she had done. She had denied her mission. She had betrayed her friends. And she had betrayed her King when she retracted her pledge. She wept. She sat in the bottom of the executioner's cart as it rumbled through the cobbled streets of Rouen, and she wept with shame. They had promised to help her, they had told her it would be hard, but in the end they would help her. "Saint Catherine, Saint Margaret," she sobbed. "Oh please help me now. . . ." She thought how Jean had kept his promise to be with her whatever happened and she cried harder, digging her knuckles into her eyes because she had not kept her promise.

She was quiet when Father Massieu and Thirache lifted her down in the prison courtyard. The English guards half carried her to her cell. She let them shackle her to the post. She extended her legs so they could fasten the leg irons. Then she sat upon the bench, her hands hanging with the heavy quiet of despair between her knees. Her head bowed. The tears ran quietly over her cheeks.

Outside the pigeons wheeled in the sunlight and all
the world was spring.

Jean de Metz knelt in the castle chapel. The hush
of evening was all about him. Two candles burned on
the altar. A hand touched his shoulder. He glanced up.
He beheld Father Massieu.

"Will it be possible, think you?"

"It will be possible. This is not a prison of the
Church, but the girl has been judged by a tribunal of
the Church, and we, the priests of that tribunal, have
access to her." He smiled faintly.

"Father Massieu, will this bring you into great
trouble with your superiors?"

"Perhaps." He shrugged. "I am under a vow of
obedience to our Holy Mother Church, as you know.
But I am only a sinful man. It is possible that a dread-
ful error is made this night by the servants of God in
the name of His Church, because we do not serve with
His compassion the world He has made, and for which
He died."

Jean rose from his knees. He genuflected without
haste before the altar. He looked searchingly into the
eyes of the priest.

"It is a great favor I have asked of you. I know
nothing of the right and wrong of this trial. But long
ago, when I brought Joan to the King, I pledged her

my knightly word that I would be with her whatever
came. And now she is alone."

"You risk your life to this end, but come. There are
no more words, and we waste the few hours of her life
that remain."

Turning, Father Massieu led the way from the
chapel. Torchlight cast red shadows in the corridor.
The rancid odor of burning pitch caught in Jean's
throat as they emerged from the cool sanctuary. The
priest took one torch from a wall bracket.

In silence they walked to the oaken door. Father
Massieu knocked three times. The bolts screeched. The
massive door swung inward. Two English guards in
the livery of the Duke of Bedford stood in their path.
At sight of the familiar black and white habit they
stepped aside. They recognized Father Massieu, but
they did not question the presence of his companion,
so many priests had visited the Maid in her confine-
ment.

Father Massieu held his torch high. As they entered
the dank passage that led to her cell, Jean felt his
stomach turn over. He gagged at the foulness of the
air. Father Massieu smiled again, the faint enigmatic
smile he had worn when he spoke of his own fate.

"One becomes accustomed to it."

"Has it always been like this?"

"Always." The priest took a key from the rope girdle
at his waist.

"Joan," he called. "Joan."

There was a stirring in the darkness beyond the flickering of torchlight. A stirring as of a young chained animal roused from sleep.

"Yes," she said. Then Father Massieu stepped forward and the light fell on the bars of her prison. He unlocked the grated door, and the light fell on her. The priest stood against the door.

"I will return for you at daybreak," he said briefly.

Jean stepped past him into the cell, and he was glad that Father Massieu had taken away the light. He knew Joan had seen him. He knew she had recognized him. Her trembling icy hands reached out for him in the dark. He held her hands tightly in his own for a minute. Then he sat down on the bench beside her. He wanted to put his arms around her because she was like a child who had got lost in the dark.

"How came you here?" she whispered.

"I found Father Massieu in the castle chapel on the afternoon of the day in Saint-Ouen. I begged this of him. He arranged to bring me with him tonight. If the Bishop finds out, he will suffer for it. But so many priests have questioned you, surely one more . . ." he broke off. "Oh, Joan, what have you done?"

"I did not know what I had done," she said unsteadily, "until you touched my hand, until I looked up and saw you there. Then I knew that I had broken my promise. I betrayed my King. But I was so frightened. They said I would have help. My lady Catherine promised that I would have help, but I was frightened, and I broke my promise. I forgot."

"And now, Joan?"

She withdrew her hands from his. She lifted them. For a moment she held his face between her hands. It was too dark to see her expression, but he knew that she was smiling at him, with the strange and radiant tenderness of another time. His throat ached with the sudden pressure of tears.

"And now?" she repeated. "Now I am not frightened. I told them when they came this morning. You see, Saint Catherine and Saint Margaret did not leave me. All that night I wept, for I thought they would never come again for I betrayed them and they were my friends."

"Did they come back, Joan?"

"Oh yes," she said joyously. "They came back. The lady Margaret wiped my tears on her veil. And she kissed me. She kissed me, and my face is so dirty. She told me that the King of Heaven understood and he sent them to comfort me for the great betrayal I made in order to save my life."

She took her hands from his face and pressed herself as closely against his side as the iron girdle and her chains permitted, as if, he thought, there was comfort to be had in his human nearness. Her voice, muffled against his habit, still rang with her passionate conviction.

"What I said in the cemetery, I said because I was afraid of the fire. If I said the King of Heaven did not send me, I should indeed lie, for He did send me. Jean, I would rather do penance once with my life than go on like this. Truly. Whatever I said, I said through fear of the burning."

He felt that she was looking up at him through the dark. He cradled her black head against his shoulder for an instant. He remembered how she had cried when she saw the slain English soldiers upon the field of battle for the first time and how for an instant then he had cradled her head against his shoulder. He felt her stiffen.

"What is it?" he said.

"It is the hour of dawn. I always know, because the air grows colder."

"Joan, do you know what day this is?"

"Yes, I know. This is the day I am going to die. My lady Catherine told me. Yet she told me by a great victory I would be delivered. I do not understand. But it does not greatly matter. I have done the things that the King of Heaven sent me to do."

"They will be coming for you presently," he said. "Joan, are your afraid?"

She nodded against his shoulder.

"Oh Jean, where will I be tonight?"

"Have you not good hope in the Lord, then, ma mie?" he asked gently.

"Oh, yes. With His help I shall be in His Kingdom." She broke off suddenly and he knew though he could not see that her eyes were shining. "Now I understand, now I know what they meant," she whispered. "They said I would be delivered through a strange victory. And they would bring me to the King of Heaven. I am delivered from the fear. Because they will come for me. I know they will. Is this the victory, Jean?"

He bent his tonsured head, and kissed her brow. He could not speak.

She nestled against him like a tired child. After a moment of silence, she said timidly, "Will it hurt very much?"

"Yes, Joan."

She shuddered. "I am not brave about that. I will cry out. But I am not afraid in my heart any more. That is the victory they promised, and they will be with me I know, and they will take me with them when it is finished."

At the end of the corridor the bolt screeched as the great door opened.

"Will you be there, Jean?"

"Yes, I will be there."

"Please stand near, as near as they will allow you. I think I will have more courage if I can see the face of a comrade."

Father Massieu appeared at the door, torch in hand.

"The Bishop and the judges will be here in one hour, Joan. Friar Ladvenu will come in a little while to shrive you. Sir Knight"—he addressed Jean—"you must go now. I will let you out of the castle by the postern gate."

Jean stood up. In the smoking torchlight, his eyes met Joan's. And his heart wept within him. She looked so young and lonely, her face streaked with dirt and tears under the tangled mop of black hair. But she was looking at him. And she was smiling. The smile lighted her gray eyes for a second like the shining of the sun on a winter sea.

"And now good-by," she said. He touched her cheek, then he turned and followed Father Massieu from the cell.

In the center of the Vieux Marché, the market place of Rouen, a high platform had been erected. Beneath it a great pile of faggots, smeared with oil and pitch and sulfur was arranged.

Thirache, the executioner, brought his cart to a halt beside it. He was dressed in a red woolen tunic and heavy black boots. He lifted Joan, whose hands were tied behind her, and carried her up to the platform. He set her gently on her feet in front of the iron stake and unbound her. Joan looked down. A hundred English men-at-arms had escorted her with mace and battle-ax to the place of execution. Eight hundred more English soldiers mingled with the people of Rouen who had come to see her die. Joan looked down at the sea of alien faces and panic went through her in a wave.

Thirache chained her to the stake.

"Joan." She looked down again and saw that Jean was standing at the foot of the scaffold, even as he had promised. He was holding something up to her. She could not reach him, but Thirache bent over and took the little cross made of two pieces of wood bound together. He gave it to her and she held it tightly. For a moment her eyes met his, then she was forced to look away because the Bishop and his entire court had arrived. They mounted a stage on the opposite side of the market place, and seated themselves.

The Bishop rose. Silence descended on the restless crowd as he began to read the sentence of death.

Joan held her little wooden cross. She looked at the Bishop. She looked down at the cart from which they had lifted her. She looked at the mule, his gray hide dappled with sunshine and his eyes half closed in the early spring warmth. She remembered how she wanted to pat him, and she looked at Thirache, who stood waiting beside her, a kindled torch in one hand. She remembered that he had understood about the mule, and she wanted to thank him for that, but she did not have time. The Bishop pointed at her.

"Do your duty," he thundered. Thirache set the torch to the faggots. Sparks flew. Blue smoke curled up from beneath the pile. Joan saw it. For a moment the terror engulfed her. She screamed.

"Joan!" Heedless of the danger he was in, Jean stepped to the edge of the scaffold. "Joan, I am here."

She looked down at him. She nodded. Her eyes brimmed with tears. She smiled.

Then she looked up into the fathomless blue of the sky. She held the little wooden cross tight. The moment had come. The moment she had dreaded so long. She screamed, but it was different now. Now it was pain.

"Joan," she heard them calling to her, Catherine and Margaret, and she cried out in joyous answer. Between her anguished screaming, she cried to them, and Jean, standing just below the raging fire, saw by her face that it was, indeed, true. They had kept their promises. They had come for her as she had told him they would.

"Saint Margaret," she called. "Oh my lady Catherine—" then suddenly violently she jerked her head away from the stake. In her soot-blackened face, Jean saw the gray eyes widen with the shock of recognition.

"Lord Jesus, Oh, Lord Jesus," she cried. Her charred slender body sagged in its chains.

Jean turned and threaded his way through the crowd and walked slowly toward the Dominican monastery. Joan, Joan, his heart wept, and still he knew with a kind of quiet exaltation that it was finished. That they had come for her as they had promised, not only her friends, but the King had come Himself to bring her into the Kingdom. He knew that this was her victory over fear. This was her great and shining victory that men would remember through all time to come. When the night was dark about them, when there was not one star above them then they would remember how the girl from Lorraine had won so great a victory.

Over Jean's head the pigeons wheeled in the sunlight and all the world was spring.